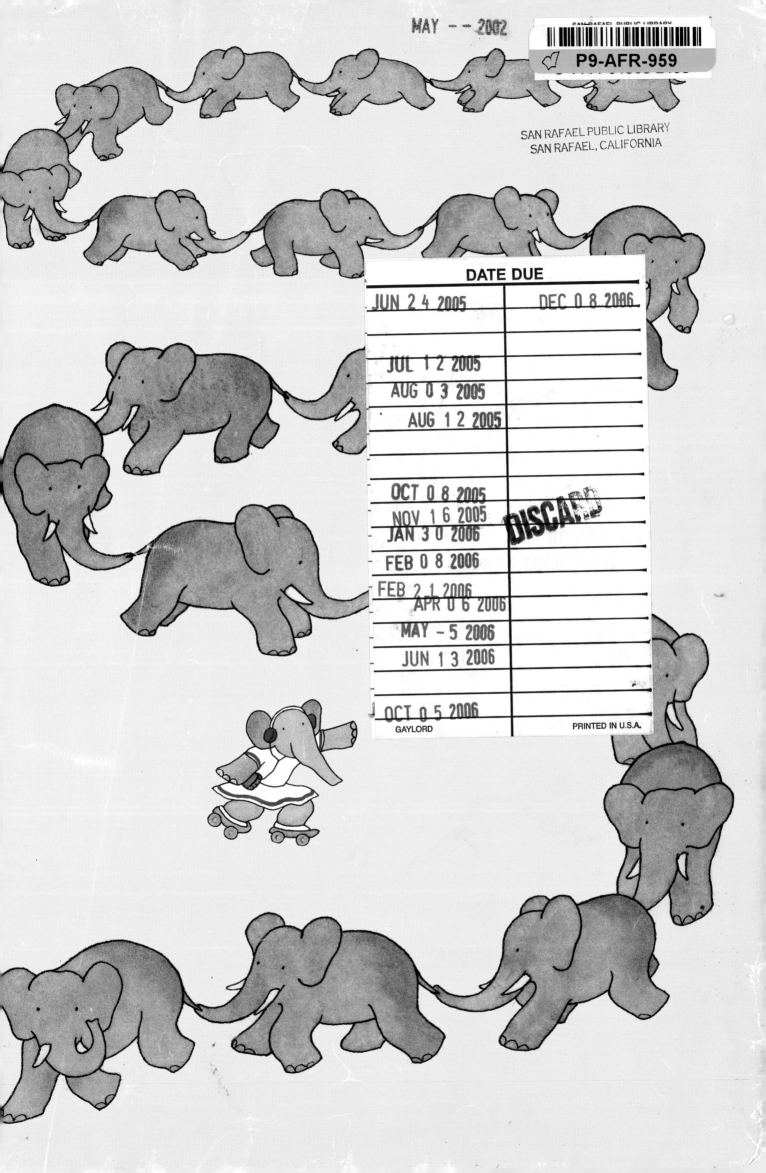

BABAR'S
LITTLE GIRL

BABAR'S
LITTLE GIRL

Laurent de Brunhoff

Harry N. Abrams, Inc., Publishers

There was wonderful news in Celesteville. Celeste was going to have another baby! Babar was hoping for a little girl so there would be just as many girls as boys in their family.

Celeste was heavy and round. She got tired easily. One day she was resting under a tree. All of a sudden, she called out to Babar, "Quick! Get Doctor Capoulosse and an ambulance. The baby is about to arrive!"

But before the doctor could get there, the baby was born. It was a girl.

The baby was named Isabelle. Celeste loved to show her off at every opportunity. Pom, Flora, and Alexander were enchanted with their new little sister, and so was everyone else.

Isabelle was an amazing baby. When she was only a few weeks old, she could already stand in her cradle. She liked to throw her toys at her brothers and sister!

Her appetite was astonishing. And from the moment she got up in the morning, Isabelle was full of energy. But often Babar was sleepy. He had spent much of the night trying to comfort Isabelle when she cried.

Soon Isabelle was starting to walk. At first she would take a few steps and fall if the other children were not there to catch her. But then one day she walked all by herself! Everyone was proud of her.

Sometimes Isabelle was very loud and her brothers and sister were exasperated with all the noise she made, shouting and blowing her trumpet. But they still played whatever game she wanted.

And sometimes Isabelle was very quiet. She loved to watch insects in the grass. The grasshopper was her favorite.

One day all the children went out for a walk. They saw a group of hippos sunbathing. One of the hippos was sitting on a turtle.

"Help! Help! I'm being squashed!" cried the turtle.

"Sir, I wonder if you could please roll over a little," Isabelle asked. But the hippo refused.

"Let's push him away," said Isabelle. And so they did.

"Thank you," said the grateful turtle.

With each passing year Isabelle's family loved her more and more. On her fifth birthday Babar and Celeste gave a wonderful party. All her friends were invited.

Because Isabelle loved music so much, her parents asked the musicians of the Royal Guard to play. The Old Lady prepared the lunch and a spectacular birthday cake.

Isabelle was overjoyed with her birthday presents—a pair of roller skates and a CD player with earphones. While out for a spin on her new skates, she noticed a cat up in a tree. She thought it was lost.

"Kitty, come down," she called. "I will help you find your home."

But the cat stayed right where it was. Isabelle waited and waited until the cat made up its mind to come down.

Isabelle held the cat in her arms and skated home. She had forgotten it was lunchtime. When she arrived Babar scolded her.

Isabelle was very upset. She hid behind a bush. Later Babar explained that she must never disappear without telling them where she was going, because everyone had been very worried.

A few days later, the whole family went for a walk in the mountains. When it was time to go home, Isabelle was nowhere to be found.

"Where can she be?" asked Celeste anxiously.

Isabelle had completely forgotten what Babar had told her. She was having a lovely time. She played hide-and-seek by herself. She walked, she ran, she skipped, and she jumped. She was very happy and sang loudly, never thinking that anyone might wonder where she was.

She wandered farther and farther until she reached the Blue Valley, a place where Boover and Picardee, old friends of the family, lived.

"I would like to go and see Boover and Picardee. They are fun. But how can I cross the river?" Isabelle wondered. She walked along the shore until she saw an old elephant in a motorboat.

"Hello, sir!" she shouted. "Could you please come and take me across?"

The old elephant was happy to help Isabelle.

   "I have taken travelers across this river for so many years that I never miss the landing, even though I cannot see well anymore," he told her.

Isabelle thanked the old elephant for the ride and hurried up to the house.

"Is anybody at home?" she called.

A moment later two gentlemen appeared at the door.

"Isabelle!" said the plump Boover.

"What are you doing here?" said the tall Picardee.

"I'm looking for someone to play with," Isabelle told them.

"Then you have come to the right place," said the two gentlemen together.

Isabelle was thirsty and hungry after her trip. Boover and Picardee gave her orange juice and some cookies.

"Would you like to play hide-and-seek?" asked Boover.

"That's my favorite game!" said Isabelle.

She hid behind the sofa. But Boover found her right away.

Isabelle ran off, looking for a better place to hide. The old house was full of surprises. Isabelle found a room covered with mirrors. She was fascinated by all the little Isabelles.

Later Picardee stood on his head and showed them some yoga. Isabelle and Boover tried it too. Isabelle was a lot better than Boover.

Then they played a game of cards.

Boover and Picardee loved jazz. Isabelle did not have her
trumpet with her, so she played the drums.
Then they taught her to tap dance.
"What a wonderful day!" cried Isabelle.

Later they went downstairs to watch television. There was Babar on the screen!

"Our little girl has disappeared," he said. "Isabelle, if you are listening, please come home right away."

Boover and Picardee were horrified. "Didn't you tell anybody you were coming here?" they said.

Isabelle began to cry. "I did just what Papa told me *not* to do," she said. "And now everyone is worried about me."

Her two friends were upset too. "Quick! Let's take Isabelle back in our car right away," said Boover.

"We can't," said Picardee. "Remember, the car is being fixed."

"Then what shall we do?" asked Isabelle.

After a moment's thought, Picardee said, "The quickest way back to Celesteville is to fly on our hang gliders."

"Surely not with Isabelle?" Boover said anxiously.

"Oh, please can we?" replied Isabelle. "I would love to fly."

From the top of the mountain they took off on their hang gliders. Isabelle rode on Picardee's back. "Hold on tight!" he warned her. Isabelle's heart was racing. She was flying like a bird. Far below was Celesteville.

"We are coming in for the landing!" cried Picardee. "Right on the terrace of the palace."

Picardee touched down nicely, but Boover was not so lucky. They had to help him down from a tree.

Boover and Picardee folded up their hang gliders. Then they kissed Isabelle goodbye.

"Go and find your brothers and sister," said Picardee. "We will tell Babar you are safe and well."

"Come and see us again," said Boover, "but do remember to tell your parents first."

Then Isabelle heard someone calling her name. She ran down the stairs and saw Arthur and Zephir.

Arthur carried Isabelle on his shoulder. Pom, Flora, and Alexander were delighted to see their little sister again.

"Welcome home, Isabelle!" cried Pom.

"Why did you run away?" asked Flora.

"We missed you," said Alexander.

After Isabelle told them what had happened, her brothers and sister wanted to hang glide too.

"You are lucky," said Pom. "All the exciting things happen to you."

But Arthur burst out laughing and said, "Isabelle, surely you don't expect us to believe *all* that."

"It's all true!" cried Isabelle indignantly.

At last Babar and Celeste were reunited with their little girl. They could hardly speak, they were so grateful to have her back. But then Babar took Isabelle on his knee and told her that she had been very naughty and disobedient.

"You have caused everyone a lot of trouble and worry," he said. "Promise me you will never do it again."

"I won't, Papa," Isabelle whispered. And, tired out by her adventures, she fell fast asleep on Babar's lap.

"Our little girl is very special," said Babar, with a smile.

DESIGNER, ABRAMS EDITION: Darilyn Lowe Carnes

The artwork for each picture is prepared using watercolor on paper.
This text is set in 16-point Comic Sans.

Library of Congress Cataloging-in-Publication Data

Brunhoff, Laurent de.
    Babar's Little Girl / Laurent de Brunhoff.
        p. cm.
    Summary: The arrival of new baby Isabelle creates much excitement
in Babar's family, particularly after she learns to walk and gets lost in
the mountains.
    ISBN 0-8109-5703-5
    [1. Elephants—Fiction. 2. Babies—Fiction. 3. Lost children—Fiction.]
I. Title.

PZ7.B82843 Babn 2001
[E]—dc21   00-44809

PRINTED AND BOUND IN BELGIUM

Harry N. Abrams, Inc.
100 Fifth Avenue
New York, N.Y. 10011
www.abramsbooks.com